top
secret

top secret

stories chosen by
wendy cooling

Dolphin

A Dolphin Paperback

First published in Great Britain in 1997
by Orion Children's Books
a division of the Orion Publishing Group Ltd
Orion House
5 Upper St Martin's Lane
London WC2H 9EA

A catalogue record for this book is available
from the British Library
Typeset by Deltatype Ltd, Birkenhead, Merseyside
Printed in Great Britain by Clays Ltd, St Ives plc
ISBN 1 85881 453 7

contents

killer sir

hazel townson

Snodger was our new art teacher, filling in for a term while Mrs Jones had her operation. Right from day one Sam and I thought he looked a pretty sinister character, but everybody else kept going on about how great Snodger was. The girls thought he was the fairest marker and the lightest punisher the school had ever known. Yet one day Sam spotted him furtively spilling this ruby pendant into an envelope and stuffing it in his drawer.

We knew all about that ruby pendant. There'd been a close-up picture of it on the news, an oval stone with three gold wiggly bits round it. A girl called Alison Agar from the next village had been wearing it when she went missing. She was headline news; swarms of police were looking for her … and all the time, there was her ruby pendant, in Snodger's desk!

Sam wanted to tell the police, but I said to hang on a bit for more proof.

'They'll never believe a couple of kids like us,' I told him, 'anyway, by the time they turn up old Snodger will have got rid of the evidence.'

So we kept an eye on Snodger. In fact, we did an in-depth study of him right through double art, and the more we found out about him, the more convinced we grew. For instance, he had an ominous red stain on his shirt cuff, plus a couple more on his jeans, and he kept taking his glasses off and staring into space with a mad look in his eyes. One eye actually kept twitching, and now and again he held his thumb out at arm's length and stared at *that*, which didn't seem normal to me. To cap it all, he actually lost his temper and accused Sam and me of spying on him, which is a persecution complex and a real sign of a psychopath.

We decided to investigate further by following Snodger home after school. He used a push-bike same as we did, so we waited for him round the back of the bike shed, then rode after him. We should have had more sense. Why didn't we realise we were very likely pedalling to our doom?

It turned out Snodger lived miles away at the back of beyond, up a miserable little lane full of puddly potholes, with two semis at the end of it. The very place for a murder!

Snodger stopped at the second semi and wheeled his bike into a shed while Sam and I settled in behind the privet to keep watch.

Snodger soon reappeared with a spade. There was a partly dug hole in the side garden which he started work on right away.

'Hey, he's digging a grave!' whispered Sam.

I had to admit it looked that way. The hole was oblong and pretty deep.

'Think it's long enough for a woman, though?'

'It is if he's chopped her up first,' declared Sam. 'Or maybe he's already buried Alison Agar, and this is for victim number two who's a bit shorter.'

So far, the newspaper hadn't mentioned a number two but there was always Pete Shaw.

Pete Shaw had been one of our classmates until a few days ago. He was supposed to have been packed off to his gran's all of a sudden, though nobody knew why. At any rate, that was the excuse old Snodger gave us when Pete stopped coming to school without a word to anyone.

At long last Snodger laid down his spade, mopped his brow, and gave his back a good massage. He obviously wasn't used to all that hard labour. Then he started dragging this bulky sack from the shed. Even from behind the privet we could see that the sack had brownish-red marks all over it.

Brownish-red marks! Like the ones on his shirt cuff and jeans!

Bloodstains!

And whatever was in that sack was just about the same size as Pete Shaw.

'We were right!' croaked Sam.

'Looks like it!'

I must admit I was pretty shaken. It's one thing to have dark suspicions, and another thing to have them confirmed before your very eyes.

Snodger was having a struggle with that weighty sack, but at last he managed to drag it to the edge of the hole and tip it in. He stood and stared down into the hole for a while with a very strange look on his face. Then he started shovelling the earth back in. He was working fast, and had replaced about half the earth when suddenly his telephone rang. He flung down his spade and ran into the house.

'Quick! Now's our chance for a bit of sleuthing!'

Sam hesitated, but I grabbed him by the arm.

'If it was you in that sack, and Pete Shaw out here, you'd want him to do something about it, wouldn't you?'

'Such as?'

'There are bound to be clues in the shed. We might even find that ruby pendant. He won't have dared to leave it lying about in school.'

We belted across the garden and into the shed. Once we'd shut the door, there wasn't much light in there.

'We should've brought a torch,' grumbled Sam. 'Fat lot of clues we're going to find in the dark.'

We were just wondering whether to pack it in when the door flew open and there stood Snodger. He must have crept up quietly on purpose, because we hadn't heard a thing.

'Well now, just what do you think *you're* doing?' Snodger demanded in bloodcurdling tones.

'Sir, we – er – our ball came over your hedge, sir! We thought it had rolled into the shed because the door was a little bit open.'

This was a brave and brilliant effort on my part, but Sam started chickening out again.

'Never mind, sir! It's only a ball so it doesn't matter; we'll leave it for now,' he gabbled wildly. 'We have to get home, you see. Our folks will be worried.'

'You followed me, didn't you?'

'Er – well, sir, we were going this way anyhow.'

'This way home?'

Snodger smiled a strangely chilling smile.

'Well, now you're here, you may as well come in. Find out how the other half lives. Teachers do have lives outside school, you know. PRIVATE lives.'

I was the nearest, and he began to propel me gently but firmly towards the house.

'You too, Watson!' he called to dawdling Sam, whose surname is actually Smith.

'We – er – really ought to be going, sir! We've got piles of homework …!'

'Nonsense! Another ten minutes won't make any difference now, and a quick snack will give you the strength to pedal home.'

Snodger's living quarters were a mess. He was always going on at us for being untidy in the art room, but he had books and dirty laundry scattered all over the place, not to mention a sinkful of unwashed dishes and a load of dirty paint brushes in a jam-jar on the sideboard. The walls were covered with these weird-looking pictures he paints, trees with eyes and mouths, and stuff like that. There were some half-finished canvases as well, propped up against the skirting-board. And I can tell you that a couple of them gave me a nasty shock. They showed a woman's body lying face down on a great marble slab, with a dagger sticking out of her back! What really turned me to jelly was that right there on the table was this whacking great bloodstained knife.

'Sit down, then!' invited Snodger, shifting more clutter off the chairs. 'I think we can rustle up some lemonade and biscuits. Or would you rather hang on for the beef stew? It's just gone into the pot.'

Needless to say, we plumped for the lemonade, but when he went into the kitchen to fetch it I whispered to Sam, 'Don't eat or drink anything; it might be drugged.'

Sam turned two shades whiter but didn't answer.

When Snodger came back with two (not three!) glasses and a plate of custard creams he gestured at his pictures and said: 'Well, what do you think, then?'

'G-great, sir!' stammered Sam.

'Yeah, great!' I lied.

'Gets rid of all my inhibitions,' grinned Snodger slyly. 'Trouble is, it's a very absorbing hobby. Doesn't leave much time for anything else.'

Like cleaning up, I supposed he meant, but then he added: 'Such as devising tortures for inquisitive kids.' He seemed to think this was very funny, but we didn't.

Then the telephone rang again. It was right there in the room, so we couldn't help hearing Snodger's half of the conversation. We found it far from reassuring.

'Yes, thanks, I did get your message ... I believe you wanted two more sacrificial victims. Well, don't worry, I've got them here now ... Oh yes, no problem! I'll easily be able to finish them off this evening ... I'll give you a ring in the morning if all goes to plan ...'

As this nightmare conversation continued, two frightening facts fell into my brain.

One: there was still no explanation for the bloodstained sack. You don't go burying pictures, however badly they might turn out. And anyway, pictures don't bleed.

Two: I suddenly remembered glimpsing the man next door peering furtively round his curtain just as we arrived. He'd looked even more sinister than Snodger and could well be Snodger's accomplice, keeping in touch by telephone so as not to show his face. That face reminded me now of one I'd seen in a library book called *The Weird World of Wizards*.

It was time to make a hasty exit!

Fortunately, Snodger was standing with his back to us, still dealing with his caller. I made frantic signals to Sam, then slowly and painfully we inched our way as far as the door. At last we started running. I have never run so fast in my life.

We had just reached the front gate as a car drew up and this dazzling blonde stepped out of it. She was a real cracker; I couldn't help giving her a second glance ... which showed me she was wearing a ruby pendant with three gold squiggles round the stone.

The rat! He'd given Alison Agar's pendant to this blonde without a qualm of conscience, and who was to say he wouldn't murder her as well, then pass it on to somebody else?

Before the woman had even realised we were there, we leapt onto our bikes and pedalled away like Milk Race winners. It was great to reach civilisation again, even the traffic jam in the High Street.

We both told our folks what was going on, but as usual they didn't believe a word we said. So I rang up Sam and suggested we went to the police right away, no messing.

'Lives might depend on it,' I pointed out.

'Yes, ours!' Sam retorted darkly. 'Dobbing on Snodger is the best way to set him on our trail with all guns blazing!'

Maybe he was right. I went to bed early instead, and had nightmares about Snodger clambering through my bedroom window with that bloodstained knife between his teeth and a revolver in each hand.

I can't tell you what a relief it was when Snodger didn't turn up for school next day. (In fact we didn't see him in school ever again. A breezy new supply teacher sailed in for the rest of the term.)

It turned out Snodger had rung the head that morning to explain that his dog had been run over and that he'd put his back out while burying the animal in the garden. He claimed he was in agony and hardly able to move.

A likely story! If he was in such agony, how did he get to the telephone? And why did we catch sight of Pete Shaw's gran that very afternoon, rushing into the head's office absolutely bursting with shattering news?

Sam and I decided that as we were the only ones with all the evidence, it might be as well to write it down in case WE ever disappeared.

So we went and bought two exercise books. We'd just finished felt-tipping our names on the fronts of them when three things happened.

First, Alison Agar was arrested for helping with a jewel robbery, part of the loot being this ruby pendant she was still wearing.

Second, there was a picture of Snodger in the local paper, getting engaged to the dazzling blonde with a ruby ring to match the pendant he'd given her for her birthday. Apparently he'd also won some art competition with a painting called 'Sacrificial Victim'.

And third, Pete Shaw came round to tell us his mum had just had twins.

the mysterious disappearances at humbug lodge

leon rosselson

The car swerved into the motel driveway and skidded to a stop. A neon sign above the office said HUM-BUG LODGE. A light shone in one window of the office. Like one eye open, thought Susan. Elsewhere, there was a darkening world. The sun had disappeared behind Humbug Mountain which loomed over them like a fearsome giant with a hooked nose. A black cloud hung menacingly overhead.

'I don't like this place,' complained Billy. 'When are we going to Disneyland?'

'When we get to California,' said Dad. 'Right now we're in wonderful, picturesque Oregon.'

'It's raining again,' said Mum.

'You said it was going to be sunny,' accused Billy. 'You said we'd come back brown as berries.'

'You can get brown in the rain,' said Dad.

'How?' asked Billy.

'Rust,' said Dad. And laughed.

He was always doing that. Making jokes no one laughed at.

Apart from that, thought Susan, as dads go, he's all right.

A short chubby man wearing a white peaked cap and grubby overalls emerged from the office. 'Hi,' he said. 'You looking for something?'

'Somewhere to stay the night,' Dad replied. 'Do you have room?'

'I guess so,' said the man. 'Follow me.'

Susan thought: there's something funny about his eyes.

Dad followed the man into the office.

Mum, Billy and Susan waited. No one spoke. A gust of wind rushed through the trees. A little to the right and behind the office, Susan could make out a gleam of water. They waited. Two minutes. Five minutes. No one spoke. Susan held her breath and waited for the scream.

'Suppose he doesn't come back,' blurted out Billy. 'Suppose –'

'Don't be silly,' said Mum heavily.

At that moment, Dad stepped out of the office waving a bunch of keys.

'There we are,' said Mum, breathing a sigh of relief. 'We mustn't let out imaginations run away with us.'

'Cabin number thirteen,' said Dad. 'Take this path to the right and it's behind the lake.'

Mum drove slowly down the path till they came to a lake surrounded by trees. A row of identical wooden cabins lined the lake. There were no lights in any of them.

'What are those birds,' asked Billy, 'swooping over the lake?'

'Bats,' said Dad.

'No, they're not,' said Susan. 'They're swallows.'

'I know they're swallows,' said Dad. 'But look at the way they're flying round and round the lake. They must be bats.' And he laughed.

'Take no notice,' said Mum. 'Just his little joke.'

'It's here,' said Dad. 'Number thirteen. Romantic, isn't it?'

'What I want to know,' said Mum, 'is why we're the only people staying here.'

Exploring the cabin didn't take long: a bedroom with twin beds for Mum and Dad, a tiny bathroom with shower and toilet, a small kitchen housing a table, four chairs, a fridge and an electric stove and a sitting-room with a TV and a pull-out sofa bed where Susan and Billy would sleep.

'Great!' said Billy. 'We can lie in bed and watch telly.'

He switched on the set. On every channel, the screen

showed a violent snowstorm. Disappointed, he switched it off.

Susan gazed out of the window. She could still see swallows circling low over the water, picking up insects. Soon they would be gone. The daylight was draining away and the wind was rising, ruffling the surface of the lake and forcing the trees to bend before it. She could see the black cloud spreading over the sky. Like a stain, she thought. A bloodstain.

'I'm starving,' complained Billy.

'Me, too,' said Mum. 'There must be a restaurant nearby.'

'Nothing for miles,' said Dad. 'I asked. But we can buy food here. They said they'd open up the store behind the office.'

'Who's they?' asked Mum.

'The chubby man and his brother. I think it was his brother. Young, bit of a bruiser.'

'Where are the women?'

'I didn't like to ask. How about bacon and eggs?'

'I don't eat meat,' said Susan.

'So you don't,' said Dad. 'Well, you can have bacon and eggs without the bacon.'

'Get some bread and butter as well,' ordered Mum. 'Milk. Tea. Tins of soup.'

'And crisps,' yelled Billy.

'You mean chips, don't you, honey,' said Dad in his phoney American accent.

'And Cokes. And chocolate chip cookies,' added Billy.

Dad opened the door. The wind swirled through it, spitting a few drops of rain into the room. A lightning flash illuminated Humbug Mountain.

'Wild night,' said Dad. And huddling himself into his anorak, he strode off into the darkness.

'Come on, you two,' said Mum. 'Help me find the pots

and pans. Then you can unpack your things and make the sofa bed.'

Fifteen minutes later, Susan was playing patience on the kitchen table, Billy was still trying to find a picture on the telly and Mum was pacing up and down and anxiously peering through the window.

'Why do I spend my life waiting for your dad to arrive?' Mum exploded.

'He's not been gone that long,' said Billy. 'I think we should complain about this telly. It's rubbish.'

'How long does it take to buy a few things from the store?' said Mum.

'He's probably been kidnapped,' said Billy.

'Don't be silly,' Mum said irritably. 'More likely he's got talking to those men. You know what he's like. Sit him down with a glass of beer and he'll gossip all night. I forgot the time, he'll say. I'll murder him when he gets back.'

Susan stared at the cards on the table. 'You shouldn't say that,' she said.

Mum looked at her, surprised. 'I didn't mean it, Susan. I just wish he'd come back, that's all.'

Again she peered through the window and still there was no sign of him. She sighed and sat down opposite Susan.

'Is the patience working out?' she asked.

'No,' said Susan. 'It isn't.'

'Oh well,' said Mum. 'Sometimes it does, sometimes it doesn't.'

Billy switched the TV off. He suddenly felt so anxious he started to chew his fingernails.

They sat there in silence, listening to the wind moaning through the trees and the rain beating on the cabin roof.

'Gives me the creeps,' Mum muttered. Suddenly she stood up. 'I'm going to fetch him,' she said.

'Mum!' wailed Billy. 'You can't leave us by ourselves.'

'You'll be all right,' Mum reassured him. 'There's nothing to worry about. He must have got chatting or something. Lock the door if you're worried.'

'Mum!' pleaded Billy again, frightened.

'Five minutes there, five minutes back. I'll be back in ten minutes I promise.'

'Say something, Susan,' said Billy.

Susan said nothing. She knew what was going to happen. She'd seen it before. In a film, was it? Or a book? The parents would go. The children would be left alone. Sometimes they were in a wood. Sometimes in a house. And always IT would be coming closer. IT – the thing that brought terror. The ogre. The monster with the hideous face. The deadly invader from another world. The madman with the axe. Nearer and nearer. Soon they would hear its great shambling footsteps. Soon it would be beating on the doors, rattling at the windows, nothing could stop it, coming nearer, breaking in, its hot breath …

Susan found herself trembling with fear.

'Ten minutes,' said Mum as she went out of the door.

They were alone. They waited. Billy suggested a game of cards. Susan shook her head. Billy started chewing his fingernails again.

'Mum isn't coming back, you know,' said Susan.

'What do you mean?'

'She isn't coming back,' repeated Susan.

Billy froze. Fear beat at his heart. 'How do you know?' he shouted.

'I just know.' Susan was calm now. Now that it had happened, the trembling fear had passed. She knew they were on their own.

Billy stared at Susan. He wanted to scream at her, to stand up and force his sister to take the words back but he couldn't speak, he couldn't move. His heart was still pounding.

Suddenly, without wanting to, he burst into tears.

Susan was startled. Her brother didn't usually cry, even when he was hurt. She went to him and, as her mother would have done, put her arms around him. 'It's all right,' she said. 'It's going to be all right.'

Billy sniffed. 'They shouldn't have left us,' he said. 'I wish we'd never come to America.'

'We have to go and look for them.'

'Not me,' said Billy. 'I'm going to bed with the covers over my head till morning.'

'We can't stay here,' Susan insisted. 'If we stay here, we'll be trapped. We've got to go out and face it.'

'Face what?'

'I don't know. That's what we've got to find out. Then there'll be nothing to be afraid of.'

'You mean you want to go to that horrible man in the office?'

For answer, Susan took their anoraks, put hers on and handed the other one to her brother. As if in a dream, Billy put it on and hand in hand they went out of the door and into the darkness.

They followed the path round the lake, trying to ignore the strange sounds of the night and the menacing movements of the swaying branches.

The office was still lit up, its one eye still open. A battered blue van was parked outside. They stood at the door, hesitating. Finally Susan pushed at the doors and pulled her brother after her.

The two men looked up in surprise. The short chubby one with the funny eyes was sitting behind the desk watching a small TV set. A younger, thickset man dressed in T-shirt and jeans was leaning against the wall, whittling a stick.

No one spoke. The children stood there, wet and shaky.

Susan stared at the chubby man, stared questioningly at his stony blue eyes.

As if understanding the question, the man grinned, put his right hand up to his right eye, then took it away again.

The children gasped. The man's eye had gone. In its place was an empty socket.

The man, still grinning, stretched out his arm and opened his hand. In it sat the glass eye. With a swift movement of his hand, the eye was back in its socket.

'Cute, eh?' said the man. 'What else can I do for you?'

Billy, plucking up courage, found his voice. 'It's our mum and dad,' he said hoarsely.

'Sure. I remember. Cabin thirteen. From England. Right?'

'We're looking for them,' Susan said. 'They came here.'

'Well, that's real strange,' said the man, 'because sure as hell I haven't seen them. Have you, Chuck?'

'Nope,' said Chuck, not moving from his position. 'I'd 'a' remembered if I had.'

There seemed nothing more to say. The children retreated into the rain. The darkness outside came almost as a relief to them. They felt as if they'd achieved a great triumph.

'Did you see what he did with his eye?' Billy said indignantly.

'It was only a glass eye,' said Susan. 'That's all.'

Billy stared at his sister. She was becoming stranger and stranger.

'Anyway,' he said, 'they were lying about Mum and Dad. They wouldn't just go off and leave us.'

'No,' said Susan. 'They wouldn't do that.'

'So?'

'Well,' said Susan, 'if they've kidnapped Mum and Dad, where would they have put them?'

Billy pointed to the wooden building behind the office. 'What about there?'

'The store,' said Susan.

They tiptoed up to the door of the building. It was locked. There were no lights anywhere. They walked round the store, trying to peer through the window.

'I can't see a thing,' said Billy.

They looked at each other, at a loss.

'Supposing –' Billy began.

'Sh!' Susan touched his arm. 'Look.'

The younger man called Chuck was coming out of the office, carrying a lantern. He opened the back doors of the blue van, then went back inside.

'Supposing,' said Billy again, 'they're going to put Mum and Dad –'

'Quick!' interrupted Susan. 'Before he comes back.'

They ran to the van and scrambled into the back. They squeezed into a corner, covered themselves with some sheets of tarpaulin and tried to make themselves as small as possible.

'What about the kids?' they heard one man say.

'They're kids,' said the other. 'What can they do?'

The back doors were shut and the two men climbed into the front of the van. The engine was started. The van lurched forward. For a while there was smoothness as the van travelled along the main road but when it turned sharp left, the rattles and bumps bruised their bodies.

Where were they going? What were the men going to do?

I wish I hadn't done this, thought Susan. But it was too late to get out now.

The van slowed down, took a sudden turn to the right, crawled forwards for a bit longer, then stopped. Susan and Billy lay still as logs, hardly daring to breathe. The car doors slammed and the men's footsteps crunched away into the distance.

They crawled into the front of the car, climbed out and looked around them. They were in a dark wood, tall trees rising far above them. An owl hooted. The rain had stopped but there was no moon visible. The only light they could see was dancing away from them, the beam of the lantern carried by the men from Humbug Lodge.

'Let's follow them,' said Billy.

They felt their way through the forest, sometimes hitting themselves against branches and the roots of trees, following the lantern in the distance. An owl hooted again and the wind shook the trees. Then there was silence, a silence so deep and soft and restful that they wished they could sink into it and sleep and sleep.

The lantern stopped moving. They crawled towards it, slowly, quietly, their hands and knees wet and sore and grimy. When they were near enough they stopped crawling and watched.

A wide track ran through the forest. At the side of the track lay two rifles.

'They've got guns,' Billy whispered excitedly.

The men were tying the end of a roll of wire to a tree at one side of the track, crossing to the other side, tying the wire to another tree then back to the first side until the wire crisscrossed the track half a dozen times.

'What now, Harry?' said the younger man, Chuck.

'Now,' said Harry, 'we wait.'

They took up their rifles and extinguished their lantern. They were gone from view.

'We'd better go back to the Lodge,' whispered Susan. 'Mum and Dad must still be there.'

They crawled along the edge of the track until they were sure they were far enough away from the men. Then they stood up, stumbled onto the track and began walking back.

'How far is it?' asked Billy. 'I'm tired.'

'Me too,' said Susan.

'It was a stupid thing to do, getting into that van,' complained Billy.

'You said –' began Susan.

'It was your idea,' interrupted Billy.

'Don't let's quarrel.' Susan took her brother's hand. 'We have to stick together.'

'What's that noise?'

A strange humming sound was coming from further along the track. They stopped walking. They could see beams of light approaching them. They looked at each other. If they deserted the track for the darkness of the forest, they would be lost. If they went back along the track, the men would catch them. Ahead of them was the unknown. They were trapped …

'I don't believe this,' said the tall man with the beard. 'Babes in the wood.'

Nervously, Susan and Billy gazed up at the circle of faces staring down at them. Susan thought of Robin Hood and his merry men (even though most of these people were women) and was reassured.

A woman detached herself from the group, came towards them and knelt down. 'Hi,' she said. 'I'm Martha. Are you lost?'

'We're looking for our mum and dad,' said Susan forlornly.

'You're English. And you've lost your ma and pa in this forest?'

And so the story came out. So eager were Susan and Billy to tell this woman everything that had happened that they constantly interrupted each other.

'And Chuck and Harry are up ahead?' asked the bearded man.

Susan nodded.

'They've got guns,' Billy explained.

'Someone must be paying them a lot of money,' said a woman's voice.

'Yes, and we know who,' added someone else.

'I guess they just don't like us hugging trees,' said the bearded man.

Billy giggled. These were funny people.

'You mean you never hugged a tree?' asked the man, grinning.

Martha stood up. 'Come on, Larry, you're confusing them. I'll take these two back to Humbug Lodge. You'd better find a way round the ambush. And don't get into any fights.'

'No way,' said the man.

Martha put her arms round Susan and Billy and shepherded them along the track. 'Don't worry about your ma and pa,' she said. 'Chuck and Harry won't have done anything bad to them. They're two dumb guys who watch too much television. But they're not evil.'

'Why have they got guns?' asked Billy.

'It makes them feel big,' said Martha. 'But I don't think they'd shoot anyone. They just want to frighten us.'

And she tried to explain why she and her friends had come to the forest in the middle of the night.

'This is an old-growth forest,' she said. 'Some of these trees are a thousand years old. The logging company made this track. At the end of it there's a grove of trees they've marked to cut down. Tomorrow morning, they're coming in with their chain saws. We're here to try and stop them.'

'What about Chuck and Harry?' Billy asked. 'What are they doing?'

'I guess Judith's right. Somebody's paying them to frighten us off.'

'Why did they kidnap Mum and Dad?' asked Susan.

Martha shrugged. 'Beats me. We'll find that out when we get back to the Lodge. My truck's on the road at the end of this track.'

Humbug Lodge was in complete darkness when they arrived. Martha shone her torch at the office building, then at the store.

'It's locked,' said Billy. 'We tried it.'

Martha took a thick stick, went over to the store and broke a window. She put her arm carefully through the hole, opened the window and climbed inside. Then she switched on the lights and opened the door for the children.

'Mum! Dad!' called Billy.

'Not here,' said Susan in alarm.

'Don't panic,' said Martha. 'I think I know where they'll be.'

She went behind the counter and dragged away a crate of beer bottles. 'Help me lift this trap door,' she said.

Together, they pulled open the trap door. A ladder led downwards and at the bottom could be seen the candle-lit faces of a nervous-looking Mum and Dad.

'Thank goodness you're safe,' said Mum.

'What kept you?' said Dad.

There were hugs and kisses and tears and complicated explanations. Susan and Billy tried to make Mum and Dad understand what had happened to them after they'd been left alone and who Martha was, and Martha tried to explain about the old-growth forest, and Dad tried to make it clear that it wasn't his fault he'd been kidnapped, and Mum said emphatically that it certainly wasn't hers.

'What happened?' asked Martha.

'Well,' said Dad. 'I'd left the store with the food I'd

bought when I remembered I'd forgotten the cokes. So I went back. I saw the men loading their rifles and looking guilty. They looked at each other and at me and I looked at them and I was feeling pretty nervous by now so I said, not meaning anything by it –'

'He will have his little joke,' said Mum.

'I said: You'll never get away with it, you know. The next thing I knew they were pointing their rifles at me and ordering me into the cellar. Of course, when Mum came looking for me, they had to put her into the cellar as well. Fortunately,' said Dad, 'because I was getting rather lonely down there.'

Martha shook her head sadly. 'Chuck and Harry,' she said, 'are so stupid. Now, are you all going to be okay?'

'I think so,' said Mum. 'And thanks.'

'Sure,' said Martha. 'I'm going back to the forest. You get some sleep.'

'Sleep?' cried Dad. 'I'm starving. How about bacon and eggs?'

'Sleep,' said Mum firmly. 'These children can hardly keep their eyes open.'

When Susan woke the next morning, the sun was streaming through the windows and bacon and eggs were sizzling in the pan. She peeped out of the window. The swallows were back and there wasn't a cloud in the sky. There was a knock at the door. Susan ran to open it.

'Hi,' said Martha.

'Come in and have some breakfast,' called Mum.

When they were all dressed and sitting round the breakfast table, Martha told them what had happened in the forest.

'Thanks to Susan and Billy,' she said, 'we skirted round the ambush and caught Chuck and Harry by surprise. In the end, they admitted someone was paying them but wouldn't say who. Hard times, they said. They needed the money.'

'Did the loggers come?' asked Susan.

'That's the best bit,' said Martha. 'We'd discovered the phone number of the boss of the logging company and we called him in the middle of the night. We told him we'd caught Chuck and Harry and knew the logging company were behind it. He denied it, of course, and we can't prove anything because Chuck and Harry are too scared to tell the truth. Anyway, he was pretty embarrassed by the whole thing and agreed to suspend logging for a while. We know they'll try again. And we'll be ready for them.'

'What about Chuck and Harry?' asked Mum.

Martha shrugged. 'We reckon a stern warning'll be enough. They'll be on their best behaviour from now on.'

'That's all?' said Dad.

'We all live round here,' explained Martha. 'In the end, we have to live together.'

'But after what they did to us,' said Mum. 'After what they tried to do to you.'

'They're not the real villains,' Martha replied. 'Just a couple of hicks trying to scratch a living. As for what they did to you, well, they asked me to apologise. Nothing personal, they said. And – get this – Harry said you're welcome to stay here as long as you like, no charge.'

'I don't believe it,' said Dad.

'Why not? It's a great place. We could take you to the forest and the river and show you wonderful picnic places and where to watch the seals playing. Think about it.'

They all went outside and looked around at the trees and the lake and the swallows and Humbug Mountain towering over them, but friendly now, not at all threatening.

'It's amazing how different this place looks in the sunshine,' said Dad.

'Let's stay a few days,' said Mum. 'It'll be a rest from driving.'

'Yes, let's,' said Susan.

Billy frowned. 'What about Disneyland?' he said.

'There'll be time to go to Disneyland,' said Dad. 'I promise.'

'Well,' said Billy, 'Okay. Only –'

'What?' asked Mum.

'You won't go off in the evening and leave us, will you?'

'Never,' said Dad. 'We'll play games and sing songs and I'll do my magic tricks.'

'What magic tricks?' asked Mum.

'You know,' said Dad. 'Like my celebrated disappearing act. It's sensational.'

And this time everybody laughed.

if pigs could fly

rachel anderson

Once upon a time, not so long ago, in a school not far from here, there sat a girl who was feeling extremely grumpy.

'Blinking flip, Joe,' said Della, who knew Joe very well because she sat right next to her. 'Flipping blink, you're a right grump today. What's up?'

'Grrumph,' Joe growled. 'Them. Grown-ups!' and she thumped her paintbrush down so that it splattered green blobs all over her own painting and Della's, and even some across the desks to Sean's. His was of a high-speed train on its way under the Atlantic to New York. Or so he said.

Sean didn't in the least mind having green blobs on his picture.

'Hey thanks, Joe,' he said as the splats landed. 'That looks just like a bit of green grass. Nice. Just where I wanted it.'

Joe ignored him. 'I'm cross,' she explained to Della, 'Because my dad left me, and my brother, and our mum, to go and live on the other side of town with his girlfriend Marcia.'

'Really Joe,' said Della. 'You're not *still* on about that?' Your dad left *ages* ago. Everybody knows. And at least you still get to see him. Sean's dad's gone to New York. He never sees him at all.' And Della thumped *her* paintbrush down on the desk. This made blue blobs scatter about the classroom. Some landed on the artwork.

'Ooh yeah, great!' said Sean. 'Little fuzzy blue birds! Just what I needed! Flying over the Altantic. Thanks Della.'

Sean lived with his nan and his auntie. He always

painted pictures of trains, planes, buses and ferries going places.

Joe said, 'Yeah, Della, I know I get to see Dad. But I don't actually *like* going there. I like staying at home with my mum. Only she keeps going off to her stupid Art Class.'

It was Della's mum who'd first suggested the class to Joe's mum. After Dad went away. Della's mum told Joe's mum she ought to get out more. 'Why not join an evening class?'

At first Mum wouldn't.

'Of course you can,' said Della's mum, who liked telling other people what to do. 'You can't stay in moping for the rest of your life.'

'I couldn't possibly leave the children,' said Joe's mum.

'Nonsense! I'd only be for a few hours a week. I know an excellent childminder, Mrs Hilda Higgenfence, on Mimosa Avenue. It'll do you good to have an interest. And if *you're* happy, then your children will be happy!'

So Mum was persuaded and, sure enough, after a while she quite liked it. She began to bring home her paintings. They were large, colourful and weird, rather like the pictures that Henry did in his playgroup. Mum hung them in the sittingroom, and in the hall and the bathroom. Henry thought they were brilliant.

Then, after a few weeks of her Art Class, as well as bringing back one of her paintings, Mum brought back bad news. The whole class was off to France on a trip.

'Why's that bad?' Henry asked Joe.

'Because she's not taking us with her,' said Joe. 'Are you, Mum?'

'It won't be for long, darlings,' said Mum.

'But what about *us*?'

'Yeah, us,' said Henry because Joe told him to agree with everything she said to make sure that Mum changed her mind.

Joe said, 'Where are we going to stay? We're not going to be dumped with Dad and meddlesome Marcia, no way.'

'No way,' agreed Henry, though he quite liked it at Dad and Marcia's because Marcia treated him as though he was two years old instead of four, and let him suck his thumb.

'You'll be staying with nice Mrs Higgenfence,' said Mum. 'You'll have a lovely time, like you always do.'

'Huh. No child *ever* has a lovely time with her,' said Joe. 'How could we have a lovely time while you're gallivanting in Paris?'

'I'll be going round art galleries looking at great paintings. You *know* you wouldn't like it.'

This was true. When she'd taken them on the bus to look at great pictures in the Municipal Art Gallery, Joe had nearly died of boredom and Henry had whined that his legs hurt.

'I'll only be gone for two teeny-weeny days, not a second more. You'll hardly even notice.'

'Two days too long,' said Joe bleakly.

'And I'll bring you back a present.'

Henry was young enough to be easily bribed. 'Present?' he repeated hopefully.

Joe said, 'What *sort* of a present?' She thought of the presents Dad gave them. They were always unsuitable, like silly dolls or fluffy toys. Marcia probably chose them.

Mum said, 'A really nice French surprise.'

Joe said, 'I hate suprises.'

Henry was pleased. But Joe stood behind Mum grumbling all the while she was packing her own things for going to Paris, and Joe and Henry's things for going to Mrs Higgenfence.

Mrs Higgenfence did not understand children even

though she'd looked after so many that she'd lost count, or so she claimed.

The saddest thing of all about being at Mrs Higgenfence's was the two blue birds in a cage in the front room. They were called budgies.

'Squark, squark, chatter-chatter,' they went all day long. It wasn't a happy sound. When Mrs Higgenfence wanted to watch television, she put a cloth over the budgies' cage.

'It stops them chattering,' she explained. 'Makes them think it's their bedtime.'

The second worst thing about being at Mrs Higgenfence's was her grey sardine sandwiches.

Joe stood miserably by the cage watching the budgies hop from perch to perch. They did not look happy. Then Joe thought about sardine sandwiches and she felt more miserable than ever. Mum had been gone for hours. She wouldn't be back till tomorrow evening.

Ever since Dad went, Joe often felt afraid that if Mum went away, she might not come back either. Henry was sitting behind Mrs Higgenfence's settee so that he could suck his thumb without being seen. He was missing Mum too.

Mrs Higgenfence came in with a large plate of grey sandwiches and two small glasses of watery orange squash.

'There's my little lovies,' she said. 'Chattering love-nothing to one another.' She was talking to the budgies. 'If only children could be so sweet-natured.'

Joe was listening by the cage. The birds weren't saying sweet nothings to one another. They were complaining grumpily about their life, stuck in the front room not even being allowed to watch the television.

'Cheep, cheep, cheep. Kids get all the luck,' twittered one budgie. 'Kids, kids, all the luck. Freedom to walk about on two legs, flap their arms about, cheep cheep. Freedom to eat crisps, munch scrunch. Eat sardine sandwiches, lovely grub.'

The other budgie agreed. 'Freedom, freedom. All the luck. Cheep cheep. Do what they like. Watch Hilda's television. No cloths put over *their* heads, cheep cheep.'

'Huh,' muttered Joe. 'So you think we're lucky! If only.'

'Now then, young miss,' said Mrs Higgenfence. 'Don't stand there moping. No time for tears, not when it's time for your tea.'

Joe said. 'I'm not moping. I'm wishing. No law against that, is there?'

She was wishing: if only she knew for certain that Mum was all right, if only she'd reminded Mum to cross the roads extra carefully, because over there in Paris, the traffic goes on the opposite side, if only Mum could be back here now, or else Joe could be there, then everything would feel all right.

'Wishing?' said Mrs Higgenfence with a snort. 'No future in it. If pigs could wish, and wishes were witches, and spoons were hawks, and knives were forks!'

Joe said, 'It's not, "If pigs could wish". It's, "If pigs could fly".'

'Come along, little madam. Eat up. You're looking a bit peaky. It's bath and early bed tonight. You too, young Henry.'

When Mrs Higgenfence was watching television, she didn't like to be disturbed by chattering budgies or grumbling children.

When Joe and Henry were in bed in the dark (which Henry didn't much care for) he whispered, 'Joe, what were you really doing to those budgies?'

'Nothing. I was just thinking about Mum and wishing pigs could fly. Because then I'd turn myself into a pig.'

And that was the moment when she realised what she must do.

Early in the morning, before Henry was awake, Joe tiptoed downstairs, lifted the cloth off the budgies' cage and whispered into it,

'Would one of you swap places with me, please? Just for a day? You be me, I'll be you?'

To her surprise, one of them offered immediately. Joe opened the cage and let the budgie out so that it could become her, and she became it. She waved her arms once or twice and found they were feathery wings.

'I'll be on my way then,' she squeaked. 'How d'you get out of this place?'

The budgie, which now looked quite like Joe, opened the window for her before stumping grumpily back to bed, just like Joe on a bad morning.

Joe hopped onto the windowsill, then down into Mrs Higgenfence's front garden. She ran along the path, faster and faster, flapping hard, until suddenly she was airborne. It was easy. She wasn't worried about leaving Henry because he'd have the grumpy budgie for company.

She flew over the next-door hedge, across the allotments and the city ring-road, then followed the dual carriageway south towards the sun. She didn't know the way to Paris but the soft spring winds wafted her along. She felt she must be flapping in the right direction when she saw the sparkle of the sea ahead and heard the screaming of gulls.

The sky over the Channel was busy. There were so many hazards to avoid – steam from ships, splashing spray, the tall masts of tankers, crisp packets and drink cans chucked overboard by holiday-makers on the ferries, porpoises and tropical flying fish who'd swum off-course. The seagulls were the most difficult to cope with. They were large, bossy, strong and greedy. They kept diving down on Joe thinking that she was a tasty titbit.

'Can't you see I'm not a crumb? You silly ignorant twits!' Joe squeaked at them. 'Bread's never blue unless it's gone mouldy. There's only one kind of food in the world that's blue, and that's plums.'

Joe had nearly reached the coast of France when she heard a squeaky tweeting behind her.

'Wait for me, wait for me!'

At first, she thought it was one of the seagulls. Then she heard, 'Wanna come too. Fly more slowly. Can't keep up.'

Joe turned her yellow beak over her shoulder and saw a tiny blue budgie, frantically flapping its dainty wings.

'Oh no, Henry, not you!' Joe squarked. 'How did *you* get here?'

'Same as you,' Henry tweeted breathlessly. 'I asked that kind blue budgie to be me. And he told me which way you'd gone.'

'You *shouldn't* have followed me. You're too small for this kind of lark,' Joe squealed, but she knew she couldn't make Henry go back on his own across the deep dark sea, not with all those hungry seagulls about.

'And *you* shouldn't have left me behind. I *knew* that other bird wasn't really you! I knew it was only pretending.'

As they neared Paris, Henry squeaked, 'How'll we know where she is?'

'Easy as pie, said Joe. 'There can't be *that* many art galleries in Paris. Mum'll be wearing her bright red jacket. So we just cruise around till we spot her. We'll check she's okay, and missing us a bit but not too much, and then we buzz off home.'

So they flew over the city following the big river upstream, then downstream. Then they flew to the top of the tall iron tower beside the river and peered down from there.

Then they flew low, flitting from tree to tree along the busy boulevards. There were far more people out and about in Paris than you ever saw in Acacia Drive. People were waving from pleasure boats. Men were selling paper kites shaped like white doves. Children were flying the kites with their families in the parks. Tourists were rushing in and out of art galleries.

Henry grew tired. When he couldn't suck his feathery thumb, he began to grizzle.

'We're never going to see her,' he sobbed squeakily. 'We'll never know if she's been missing us properly.'

They flew down to the ground so that Henry could rest under a bench where some Dutch tourists were opening their baguette sandwiches. Joe pecked around under them for fallen bits.

The moment she found the first crumb, a pigeon landed right beside her.

'Why hello there!' it cooed, almost as though it knew her. Another pigeon joined it, blinking its beady eyes. Then a whole flock bobbed round, inspecting them.

'Not Parisians, surely?' cooed the first pigeon.

'No,' squeaked Henry. 'I'm Henry. From 34 Acacia Drive.' Mum had taught him to say his address, almost before he could speak, in case he ever got lost.

'Thought not,' cooed one of the pigeons. 'Japanese pigeons, are you?'

'No, they're Americans, must be,' decided another. 'Look at their bright colours.'

'You wouldn't *believe* the visitors we get over here. Indians, Icelanders, Germans, Goans, Tongans and Tahitians.'

'Actually, we're not pigeons at all,' trilled Joe. 'We're temporary budgerigars. And we're looking for our mum, to check up on her, to see she's crossing the roads carefully. And missing us.'

'Enough, but not too much,' Henry squarked.

'Searching for a mum, eh? Well, fancy.'

'What does she look like? Anything like you two?'

'Got a red coat,' tweeted Henry.

'Probably carrying her sketch book because she's very keen on great art,' Joe squarked.

The first pigeon purred softly, 'We'll find her for you.'

'In just a quick tickety-boo,' cooed another kindly.

At once, the flock rose in a flurry of beating wings. Joe watched them circle round the top of a church, then spread out for the search.

Joe and Henry hung around by the litter bins pretending to be sparrows until one of the pigeons returned.

'Found her!' it cooed. 'Over there! Red jacket. Alas, no food on her. Got presents in her bag though. A bird-kite, and a model of the Eiffel Tower. Nothing edible. Worst luck. Ah well. Nice to have met you. Enjoy your day. Bonne chance. Au revoir.'

Joe and Henry perched on the edge of the litter-bin and watched their mum carefully. She was outside a gallery with the rest of her Art Class. She was chatting to the others about the pictures they'd just seen. She didn't seem to be missing them one bit. Joe could see that perhaps the Art Class wasn't such a bad thing if it made Mum smile so much.

Joe started cheeping loudly from the rim of the litter-bin to attract attention. But Mum didn't recognise her voice and took no notice.

The teacher lead the group round one gallery after another. Joe and Henry followed at a distance. They didn't enjoy it at all.

'How many more pictures?' Henry cheeped wearily.

Mum looked really cheerful. She didn't seem to be

missing Joe and Henry one bit. But then, just as the group and their teacher were climbing back onto their coach, Joe heard Mum say to one of the other students,

'D'you know, I'm glad it's time to leave. I'm so looking forward to seeing my two little chicks again!'

'Quick, Henry!' Joe squeaked. 'We better get flapping if we're going to get home before she does.'

It seemed longer going home – across the big fields of Northern France, back over the Channel, up the M2, then the A1. Joe let Henry travel in her slip-stream so he was protected from the head winds. He was almost sleepflying most of the way.

They landed on Mrs Higgenfence's windowsill just as Mum's taxi was turning into Mimosa Avenue. Joe tapped on the glass. The real budgies let them in. They quickly changed places.

The budgies hopped back into their cage. 'Thank goodness for some decent bird-seed for a change,' they cheeped.

'And a bit of peace and quiet under our nice dark cloth.'

'And no more bedtime baths.'

Mrs Higgenfence had prepared sardine sandwiches and watery orange squash for Henry and Joe. She made their mum a cup of weak tea.

Mum held out her arms. 'My darlings!' she said. 'Have you been all right?'

'Why, upon my word,' said Mrs Higgenfence. 'They've been so good, I hardly even knew they were here.'

When Joe unwrapped the present Mum had brought her, she tried to look surprised, even though she already knew it was a white paper kite shaped like a dove.

As Henry unwrapped his surprise, Mum said, 'That's a model of the Eiffel Tower. One day, when you're old enough, I'll take you up it.'

Henry was about to say he'd already been there. Joe
nudged him. Instead, he said, 'Thanks Mum. It's nice.'

Mum said, 'And thank you both for letting me go. I've
had a fantastic time. And I've been so inspired, I'm
moving into my new blue phase of painting.'

'Oooh good,' said Henry. 'I like blue.'

Joe said, 'Well, if *you're* happy, then *we're* happy. By the
way, Mum, d'you think I could join the five-a-side
football team? Della plays. So does Sean. And Della says
I'd like it.'

seal song

jean richardson

Ben had the top bunk – and the view. When he woke up he could see the sea just by turning his head on his pillow. True it was a long way off – a sliver of blue on the horizon – but only the marshes came between the sea and the cottage where he was staying with his cousins.

Ben was used to the kind of sea that came tamely up to the prom twice a day. The sea here was different. When the tide went out, it left miles of sand scored by creeks where the water was always deep. When it came in, it was in a tearing hurry, racing across the shore in a sheet of water that could be treacherous.

There were warnings about not getting cut off by the tide. 'Some people are so stupid,' Hetty said. 'And so lazy,' added her brother Nick, who was into bird-watching and conservation. 'They can't even be bothered to walk. Serve 'em right if they drive into a creek.'

The cousins were older than Ben and knew all about the sea, birds, ways across the marshes, and sailing. They'd grown up with the sea on their doorstep. They didn't mean to show off when they said things like, 'Did you see that tern?' or, 'There's more ringed plovers this year.' Ben couldn't even recognise a seagull.

'There aren't any seagulls in London,' he said crossly, but this started a lecture on how far inland gulls actually went. As if Ben cared!

Nick took Ben sailing. He enjoyed it until they headed for the open sea. The waves slapped at the flimsy planking and he kept forgetting to duck, so that the boom nearly knocked him overboard. It was safer to look at boats in the harbour, where the wind made metallic music in the masts and men in shorts called cheery greetings as they eased their boats into the water.

The rickety landing stage was also used by the local boatmen for their trips to Seal Island, which was cut off from the mainland at high tide. A colony of seals sunbathed on its beaches or did aquabatics for the visitors. Ben's cousins had been to the island many times, so they weren't keen to waste pocket-money on going yet again.

'But I've never seen a seal,' Ben pleaded. He didn't share Nick's passion for birds, but seals were different. Every time he passed the board with the times of the day's trips, it tugged at him. He thought of offering to pay for one of them, but if he asked Nick, Hetty would be hurt and then they would quarrel. There were family arguments every day and Ben, who hated shouting and scrapping, didn't want to provoke another one.

Aunti Di came up with the solution. She offered Ben a choice of treats, and although he knew that Nick wanted to go to the nature reserve and Hetty to a stately home that did scrumptious teas, he chose Seal Island.

The only drawback was the weather. After nearly a fortnight of blue skies, several days of gusting winds were followed by rain and a sea fog that blotted out the marshes.

'There's no point in going if you can't see,' said Hetty. 'You need a sunny day to see the seals basking on the sand. They lie there snoozing and then flop into the water to take a look at the boat. They're very nosy.'

Soon there was only one day of Ben's holiday left. At ten the mist began to dissolve. By noon the sky was cloudless.

The small boat seemed overloaded with passengers. 'It's quite safe,' said Auntie Di, sensing Ben's unease. 'The boatmen are all locals. They've been doing these trips for years.'

Their boatman, a sunburnt youth in shorts and a scruffy T-shirt, seemed more interested in his girlfriend than the boat. She was wearing a black nylon suit that fitted her like a skin. 'It's a wetsuit,' said Auntie Di. 'They're for underwater swimming or water-skiing.'

As she spoke, a motorboat sheered past them in a whoosh of spray. The skier careered across their wake and waved to the girl as he shot past.

Ben thought it looked marvellous if scary, but Nick was furious.

'Cretins! Sometimes the seals can't get out of the way in time. Some have even had their heads sliced off by the tow rope.'

The boatman overheard him. 'Don't do no harm,' he said. 'Lot of fuss about nothing.'

'You wouldn't say that if your head was cut off,' retorted Hetty angrily.

'Who told you that?' said the youth. 'Lot of rubbish. There's other things harms seals beside speed-boats. Its head was probably pecked off by a bird. Great scavengers, birds.'

'Birds don't kill seals,' said Nick scornfully. The other passengers had fallen silent. Ben sensed they were on Nick's side.

'Look, there's a seal over there,' said the girlfriend. Cameras and binoculars swung in the direction she was pointing.

Ben glimpsed a sleek head the size of a small dog cresting the waves before it dipped out of sight.

The boat churned on, passing banks of sand visible above the shallow water. 'They like to sit there sunning theirselves,' said the boatman, but the sandbanks were deserted.

'You're unlucky,' said Auntie Di. 'We've seen as many as fifty on the sandbanks. They often plop into the water and come quite close.'

'Can we go round the point?' asked Hetty. 'There could be some round the other side.'

'No time,' said the boatman. 'You can walk round there if you like, but I've got a return boatload to pick up.'

'Expect they've gone round there to get away from him,' said Nick loudly. The youth revved the engine noisily.

'I'm dying of thirst,' said Auntie Di as soon as they landed. 'Let's make for the café.'

They trekked up a slope of sun-bleached sand that trickled into Ben's trainers, scratching his feet.

'I'm not going back on the boat,' Nick said. 'I can't stand that creep. I felt like pitching him overboard.'

'I bet that's why there weren't any seals,' said Hetty. 'Why should they lie around to make money for people who don't care what happens to them.'

'Animals are so long-suffering,' said Auntie Di. 'It's just as well they don't start trying to get their own back on us.'

'At least they don't cull them here,' said Nick. 'We're spared all that planned slaughter.'

They walked on in silence. Who could possibly think of killing anything on such a beautiful day. Ben trailed behind, thinking about the seals. Seeing them had been the whole point of the trip.

The café was crowded. Nick and Ben piled in and after a bit of elbowing emerged with beakers of something pale and acid.

'Anything's welcome,' said Auntie Di. She and Hetty had collapsed on the sand. The boys sprawled beside them.

'I'm walking back,' said Nick. 'I've always meant to do that walk along the ridge.'

'Not on your own you're not.' It was Auntie Di's no-argument voice. 'I don't feel up to walking that far, so I'm definitely going back on the boat. What about you two?'

'I don't think I want to walk.' Hetty was lying back with her eyes closed. 'I hate that creep, but I like being on the boat. Perhaps it won't be him.'

Nick looked cross. Ben, who was still thinking about the seals, realised that they were waiting for him to decide. He would rather have gone back on the boat too, but he sensed that Nick wanted him to say he would walk. If he didn't, there'd probably be a row.

'I'll come with you,' he said.

'Okay. Let's go.' Nick sprang up before his mother could say another word. He strode off towards the summit of the point, leaving Ben to trail after him.

'Do we have to go straight back?' he asked when he finally caught up with Nick. 'I wanted to go round to the other side … to see if there were any seals.'

'There isn't time. The tide's coming in.'

Ben felt indignant. It was thanks to him they were walking back, and it might be his last chance ever – well, at least until next year – to see the seals. Nick could do his walk any time.

'Just a quick look,' he said. 'It wouldn't take long.'

'It's too dangerous. Once the tide turns, the sea comes in very fast. We could easily get cut off. You wouldn't be much good if we had to swim.'

That did it! Trust Nick to point out that Ben wasn't much of a swimmer. He was all right in the baths at home, where there weren't choking waves or horrid things to step on. Ben was fed up with being bossed about by Nick just because he was four years older. As though a few minutes would make all that difference.

'Well I'm going to have a look,' he said defiantly. 'I'll catch you up.'

'Don't be silly,' said Nick in his school-prefect voice. 'You don't understand the tide. It's not something you can play about with.'

'I'll only be a few minutes,' Ben shouted, running back before Nick could stop him. I'd like to see how Nick would make out in London, he said to himself. As though I won't see the tide coming in!

They'd been climbing up the side of a small gully, and now Nick had disappeared Ben felt like the first man on the moon. Moonboots might have coped more easily than his trainers with the hot shifting sand and the muscular grasses that wrestled with his legs.

When he got to the top, yet another dip lay between him and the sea. He was tempted to turn back, but he didn't want to admit defeat, though he could see why most people stayed on the beach. It was like trekking across the Sahara.

When he heard the voice, he thought it must be coming from a transistor. But the song was not at all like the usual kind of pop music. Although Ben couldn't catch the words, it filled his mind with the sea. It had the shock of cold water, the swell of the waves, a salty tang. Ben wasn't sure he liked it, but it led him on … almost against his will.

The singer was lying on an arc of sand at the foot of the slope. Ben thought at first it was the girl from the boat, because she too was wearing a black wetsuit. She went on singing until Ben was only a few feet away. Then she turned her head and looked up at him.

'Hi.'

'Hi,' said Ben. Her short dark hair curled in a damp tangle and she had a snub nose and eyes that sparkled like wet pebbles. The sleek wetsuit fitted her like a glove. She was younger than the girl on the boat – about Hetty's age, Ben guessed – and much prettier. He looked round to see if she was with friends, but there was no one else in sight.

'I'm looking for seals,' he said, feeling he should explain what he was doing there. 'I came on a seal trip, but we didn't see any.'

'There are lots around,' said the girl. 'Perhaps you didn't look in the right place.' She had a curious accent. Ben decided it must be foreign.

'I heard you singing,' he said. 'You've got a super voice.'

The girl smiled. 'I always sing when I'm happy,' she said.

Ben looked out to sea. 'I'm staying with my cousins. Today was my last chance to come to Seal Island. I have to go home tomorrow.'

'I know where there are lots of seais,' said the girl. 'Shall I show you?'

Ben had been told never to go anywhere with a stranger, but the girl didn't seem like a stranger. 'Is it far?'

'No. Just the other side.' She pointed.

Ben was tempted. It was his last chance and the tide had only just turned. It took six hours to come right in.

'Okay. But can we go now.'

The girl stood up and pattered across the sand. Her wetsuit covered her feet too, making them look like fins. They made a slip-slap sound and she moved so fast that Ben could hardly keep up with her.

'Wait a moment,' he called. 'I want to take my shoes off.' He strung his trainers together and hung them round his neck. His feet could feel the ribbed pattern left by the waves and he kept his eyes down to avoid treading on anything nasty.

They had reached the shallows where waves curled across the damp sand. The girl seemed to be walking out to sea. Ben called after her: 'Where're we going? I don't want to go for a swim.'

'Follow me. It's not deep, and we're nearly there.'

Although Ben was now surrounded by water, there was firm sand only inches down. The girl obviously knew the way and Ben felt it was chicken to turn back. He glanced up. Ahead was a small island with dark shadows on it.

'There they are,' called the girl, and Ben saw that the shadows were seals. The girl had begun to sing again, and her voice drifted in and out of the sound of the waves. I bet Nick and Hetty have never been as close to seals as this, Ben thought. Perhaps I can touch one.

The girl had reached the island, but suddenly disappeared. One moment her slim black figure was outlined against the horizon, the next there were only dark shapes that slid into the sea at Ben's approach. Perhaps she'd joined them in the water. She must be an expert swimmer to need a wetsuit.

By the time Ben reached the island all the seals had gone. He looked for the girl in the surrounding water, but the sleek heads that reared above the waves all had bristling moustaches. He shouted 'Where are you?' but there was no reply.

Then he realised how far at sea he was. If he hadn't known about the sandbank, he'd have thought that he was completely cut off from the shore. Foam-crested peaks dipped down into chilling, snot-green troughs. The sky too was changing colour and the horizon was smudged with mist.

Suddenly Ben felt alone and afraid. The water was only just above his ankles, but as he began to walk back it deepened at an alarming rate. He began to imagine dangers lurking on the bottom: slimy stinging jellyfish, scuttling crabs, squidgy seaweed, broken glass … He stopped, balanced on one leg and put his trainers on. They filled with water, weighing his feet down but at least protecting them.

Then without warning his front foot began to sink. He managed to pull it clear and tried another direction. The same thing happened. Somehow he'd strayed on to a patch of mud. There were places like this on the marshes – Hetty rather liked them – where a squelchy, slippery blackness tried to suck you down. The only firm path led back to the island. The water was almost up to his waist as he retraced his steps.

The crest of the island was still above the waves, but for how long? It would be completely covered at high tide. Would he be missed before then? Would Nick wonder where he was and raise the alarm? Or would he think Ben had gone back some other way?

The mist had shortened the horizon and the air was now cold and damp. Ben thought longingly of the two frayed sweaters and old parka that Auntie Di had insisted on stuffing in her basket in spite of the sun.

He wondered what had become of the girl. Was leaving him stranded her idea of a joke? But why? He hadn't done her any harm.

When a dark head surfaced, he thought for a moment that she'd come back to rescue him, but it was only a seal, soon to be joined by several others. Ben had the uncomfortable feeling that they were laughing at him. Now it was their turn to watch a human suffer.

He was beginning to shiver, and although he waved his arms around and jumped up and down, he didn't feel any warmer.

By now the shore had vanished into the mist. If there had been anyone there, they wouldn't have seen Ben. His teeth were chattering and he had to keep shifting his feet to reassure himself they were still there. The spray must have affected his watch, because it still showed mid-afternoon though it felt as though he'd been marooned for hours.

And then he heard it, a faint sound at first but growing louder as the boat came nearer.

He shouted 'Help! Help!' as loudly as he could, but his voice faded into the mist.

'Help! Help!' He tried to project his shouts across the

waves, but they only went a few yards before being swallowed up by the sea.

Although he could hear the engine, he couldn't see the boat, and he fancied that the sound was now curving away from him. It might be his only, his last, chance, because bigger waves were now poking him under the arms and he couldn't stand up much longer.

He called again, and this time his shout billowed out into the mist. For suddenly a louder, stronger voice was also calling for him. It must be the girl! She hadn't abandoned him after all.

A small fishing boat loomed in sight, and one of the men jumped overboard and waded towards Ben.

'You've had a lucky escape,' he said gruffly, as he swung Ben over his shoulder and almost threw him into the boat. 'Lucky we heard you. We usually stay further out, to avoid the sandbanks.'

Ben was too exhausted to reply as he fumbled into the smelly jersey and creaking waterproof that was the only spare clothing they had on board. Needles of spray stung his face as he crouched in the bottom of the boat. His lips tasted salt and waves hammered at the planking as though the sea was still trying to claim him.

'Lots of seals around,' said one of the fishermen, but Ben didn't want to know or look. He'd had enough of seals.

good as gold

jean ure

O h, really, Nicola!' Nicola's mum had just come into the sitting room and skidded halfway across the floor on a skateboard. She looked at Nicola, crossly. 'How many more times do I have to tell you? PUT YOUR THINGS AWAY AFTER YOU!'

'We're playing with them,' said Nicola.

'You do not play with skateboards in a sitting room!'

'We do,' said Nicola. 'we're using it as a car transporter. Aren't we?' She turned to Tim, who nodded. 'We're playing motorways,' said Nicola.

'Well, don't play motorways! I could have broken my neck. Play something else.'

'All right,' said Nicola. She was always ready to oblige. 'We'll play car thieves.'

'And play it quietly. You're giving me a headache.'

Heavens! How grown-ups did nag. I shall never nag, thought Nicola, when I am grown up.

Nicola's mum left the room. Nicola and Tim settled down to play at car thieves. *Quietly.*

'I'll be the car thief,' said Nicola, 'and you can be the man whose car gets stolen.'

Immediately, Tim cried, 'I don't want to be the man whose car gets stolen! I want to be the car thief!'

'Well, you can't be,' said Nicola, ' 'cos I'm going to be.' Tim was younger than she was. He had to do what she told him. 'Just shut up, you'll give Mum a headache.'

Tim stuck out his lower lip.

'Go over there,' said Nicola, pointing to a corner of the room. 'That's your office and you're a person working in it. This'll be the street, and I'll be the thief walking along it. In a minute I'm going to steal your car and you're going to start shouting … help help!' cried Nicola. 'Someone has half-inched my car!'

There was a silence.

'Well, go on!' said Nicola.

Mumbling to himself, Tim moved across to his office.

'Now I'm going to steal Rollsy,' said Nicola, 'and you're going to come rushing out and –'

'No!' Tim screamed and made a dive for his favourite car. 'You can't steal Rollsy! Steal another one!'

'I can steal whatever I want … I'm a *car thief*.'

Nicola lunged. Tim, in his panic, tripped over the skateboard. Nicola hurled herself at him. Locked together, they rolled about the room.

'Gimme!'

'Shan't!'

'If you don't give it me I'll – *ow*!' yelled Nicola, as Tim kicked out.

'Can't get it, can't get it!'

Tim fled madly across the room. Nicola, incensed, tore after him. CRASH went Rollsy, flying out of Tim's grasp and bouncing off the wall into a vase of flowers. SMASH went the vase of flowers into the fireplace.

The door was thrown open.

'What are you doing *now*?' cried their mum.

'He kicked me,' said Nicola.

'Yes, 'cos she tried to steal Rollsy!'

'That was the *game*, dummy!'

'I thought I told you to play quietly?' said their mum. 'Look what you've done! You've broken my vase! What a couple of perfectly beastly brats you are!'

Nicola and Tim shuffled closer together for protection.

'You wait till your father rings! I'm going to tell him just how bad you've been!'

Their dad was away for a week on a business trip: Mum was always rotten to them when Dad was away. Today she had been specially rotten. At breakfast she had yelled at them for eating with their mouths open. She had just gone on yelling all day. At tea time she yelled at them for kicking each other.

'Like a couple of barbarians! Can't you ever behave in a civilised fashion?'

After tea, Tim went into the garden to play with his football. Nicola went upstairs to put a record on the record player that her dad had given her when he changed to CDs. Nicola's favourite record was Wham Bam Slam by a group called the Noise Machine. Nicola loved it. She loved noise of any kind. She turned the volume up really loud so that the neighbours could hear.

'Wham bam

That's what you do to me!' sang Nicola, along with the music.

'Wham bam slam

You –'

'NICOLA!' The door burst open. Nicola's mum burst in. 'Turn that dreadful racket down!'

The Noise Machine dropped to the merest whisper.

'For heaven's sake!' snapped Nicola's mum. 'What's the matter with you? Do you think the entire neighbourhood wants to hear?'

Nicola felt hurt. Why shouldn't she share her music with the neighbours? If she enjoyed it, then obviously other people would. Why was her mother so mean?

Five minutes later, Tim came upstairs, sobbing.

'What's she done to you?' said Nicola.

'She's going to stop my pocket money,' blubbered Tim. 'Just 'cos I kicked the ball and it went through the window!'

Their mother's voice came shrieking up the stairs.

'It's your own fault! I've told you often enough … don't kick that ball up this end of the garden!'

'I couldn't help it,' wept Tim.

'Of course you couldn't,' said Nicola.

Fancy expecting a poor little six-year old boy to remember which end of the garden he was supposed to kick his football in! Grown-ups were so unreasonable. Always making rules and regulations. Don't do this, don't do that. Don't make a noise. Don't swing on your chair. Don't talk with your mouth full. Don't scuff your shoes. Don't answer back. Don't pick at your food. Don't leave your things lying around. It was difficult to know what you *could* do.

Practically nothing in this house, thought Nicola; not if you were a child.

'Wish I were grown up,' she muttered. 'Do what I like then.'

One thing she certainly wouldn't do was bully poor little innocent children who were only trying to be happy.

'Beastly horrible brats!' bawled their mother, up the stairs.

Honestly, thought Nicola, it was disgraceful. She would never carry on like that when she was a grown-up.

When Nicola woke next morning the clock by the side of her bed said ten minutes past nine. Normally she would have burrowed back again down the bed and waited for her mum to call her.

'Nicola! Are you going to sleep all day?'

This morning, it seemed to her that she ought to get up. After all, someone had to lay the table and make the breakfast and do the washing up and vacuum the hall and dust the house and prepare the dinner.

Nicola got dressed and went down to the kitchen. She laid the table. She put the kettle on. She went out into the hall and called up the stairs.

'Are you two going to sleep all day?'

Then she went back to the kitchen and made the toast. There was still no sign of Mum and Tim. Nicola tutted. She went back out to the hall.

'Your breakfast is on the table! How many more times do I have to tell you? Will you please get up!'

Really! It was so inconsiderate. What did they think she was? A maid-of-all-work?

The toast was cold by the time Mum and Tim appeared. Mum said it tasted leathery. She said she couldn't eat it. Tim whined that his hot milk had skin on it. Nicola felt like boxing their ears.

'I have no sympathy with you. You should have come when you were called. As for you, Angela –' she looked crossly at Mum – 'you can either eat that toast or go without. I've had more than enough of your moaning!'

Mum pulled a face. When she thought Nicola wasn't looking she tore off a chunk of toast and lobbed it across the table at Tim. Tim promptly flicked the skin off his milk at her. The skin landed with a *flump* on top of the butter. Nicola was outraged. What a way to behave!

'Tim!' she said. 'Stop that this instant! And you, Angela. You're old enough to know better.'

Mum pulled another face. A rude one, this time. Nicola felt a strong temptation to smack her.

After breakfast they both went racing out into the garden, leaving Nicola to do the washing up. Neither of them made the least attempt to help. All they ever thought about was themselves.

They had been in the garden for about three seconds when the noise began. First it was Mum, shouting: 'Do what I tell you or I won't play!' Then it was Tim, screaming: 'I don't want to play your way, I want to play my way!' Then it was Mum, then it was Tim, then it was both of them together, bawling and bellowing at the tops of their voices.

Nicola wrenched open the back door and went running out.

'Be quiet, the pair of you! How dare you make all this noise on a Sunday morning? We'll have the neighbours complaining!'

Mum pouted and Tim picked his nose. Nicola smacked at him.

'Stop doing that, you repulsive little beast!'

At dinner time Tim refused to eat his greens and Mum upset a glass of Coke all over Nicola's clean tablecloth. At the end of the meal, without waiting to ask permission, they both scrambled down from their chairs and went rushing to the door.

'Where do you think you're going?' said Nicola.

'Going to watch television,' said Mum.

'Well, that's just where you're wrong!' said Nicola. 'You can both stay and help with the washing up. I'm sick of doing all the work round here!'

Tim immediately started grizzling: 'We'll miss the programme!' Mum, in a sulk, swept the dishes off the table and broke two of the best dinner plates.

'*Oh*!' Why are you so *clumsy*?' cried Nicola, exasperated.

They didn't care. Either of them.

'You're spoilt,' said Nicola. 'You take everything for granted.'

After watching television – and quarrelling because they both wanted to sit on the same bit of sofa – they went back out into the garden. Now, perhaps, thought Nicola, she could put her feet up and have a bit of a rest.

She had had her feet up for almost a minute when the back door burst open and Tim went tearing along the hall with Mum in hot pursuit. Mum was dangling a worm from her fingers. As she ran she chanted: 'I'm going to get you, I'm going to get you!' Tim was shrieking; dreadful ear-splitting shrieks that ripped through Nicola's aching head like a power drill.

Nicola started up from her chair. All along the hall carpet and up the stairs was a trail of muddy footprints. Nicola put her hands on her hips.

'You two! Come down here! I want a word with you.'

Tim appeared at the head of the stairs. He took one look at Nicola and fled. Nicola thought, but could not be quite certain, that she caught the words, 'Old cow's in a mood again!'

I'll give them mood! thought Nicola.

By the time she had scrubbed the muddy footprints off the carpet, it was time for tea. Mum and Tim sidled cautiously down the stairs.

'You just wait till your father rings,' said Nicola. 'I'm going to have a word with him about you two!'

Next morning Nicola woke up feeling more like her usual self. She took one look at the clock and instantly dived back beneath the duvet. No need to get out of bed until Mum called up the stairs that breakfast was ready!

And then she thought, well … maybe just for once Mum might like it if she didn't have to call her. Maybe she might like it if Nicola laid the table? And maybe if she got up a bit earlier the toast wouldn't be cold. It was horrid when it was cold; all hard and leathery.

Mum was really surprised when Nicola appeared in the kitchen and started laying the table.

'Thank you, Nicola,' she said. 'What a kind thought!'

Tim, of course, didn't appear until he had been yelled at three times and poor Mum had almost lost her voice.

'That is just so *thoughtless*,' said Nicola. 'Mum goes to all this trouble to get your breakfast and you just roll about in bed like a slug.'

Tim blinked. So did Mum.

'Next you'll be complaining,' said Nicola, 'that your milk's got skin on it.'

'Yes, it has,' said Tim. 'Ugh! I loathe skin!'

'If you got up when you were told,' said Nicola, 'there wouldn't be any.'

Tim scowled and prodded fretfully at the skin with a finger. Milk promptly went slurping over the side of the mug.

'Now look what you've done!' scolded Nicola. 'All over Mum's clean tablecloth!'

'Don't worry,' said Mum. She sounded quite amused. Why wasn't she cross with him? 'It'll wash.'

'That's no excuse. He ought to be more considerate.' Nicola looked at Tim, severely. 'I hope you're going to put your toys away today and not leave them lying around for Mum to trip over.'

Tim stared at her, open-mouthed. Mum laughed.

'I seem to remember my mum saying exactly the same thing to me ... put your toys away after you! And of course I never did.'

That evening, Dad rang. Tim and Nicola listened anxiously as Mum talked to him.

'Tim and Nicola?' she said. (Tim and Nicola held their breath.) 'Oh, good as gold! Nicola actually laid the table this morning without being asked. And Tim put his toys away! I hope you're going to bring them back a present each ... I think they deserve it.'

the skate gang

andrew matthews

Bone was thin and thin meant fast. He went everywhere on his super rollerskates with their bright red rollers. There was no fat on Bone to slow him down. His ears didn't stick out to catch in the wind. He went so fast on his skates that he was the fastest kid in town. He went so fast that his red, peaked cap blew off unless he wore it back to front.

Bone was so thin he could zip between crowds of shoppers without bumping into anyone. He never got wet when it rained because he dodged between the drops. Bone's ribs were so bony that he could play tunes on them. When he tapped them with a pencil, they went PANK! PUNK! PONK! like a xylophone. Bone was thinner than a pencil and bonier than a dinosaur.

'I can't understand it!' moaned his mum. 'The boy eats like a horse! He eats like two horses!'

It was true. No matter how much Bone ate, he never put on weight. His secret was that he used up so much energy, the food he ate never had a chance to turn into fat. Bone changed food into speed.

Bone was leader of the Skate Gang. The other members were Omar and Lucy. Omar could spin round on his skates until he was a blur. Lucy could skate faster than a falling star. But Bone was tops – he made Omar and Lucy look slow.

One Saturday morning, Bone's mum sent him round to visit his gran to see if she needed any shopping doing. Bone's gran was great! She was round with twinkling eyes and a smile like a warm oven. She liked a good laugh and made the best jam sponge in the universe.

As soon as Gran opened her door that Saturday, Bone could tell that something was wrong. Gran's smile was as droopy as a toddler's nappy.

'Gran!' cried Bone. 'What's the matter?'

'It's my old tabby tomcat Percy,' Gran said glumly. 'He's been out all night and he's not back yet.'

'Maybe he's lost,' said Bone.

'Percy never gets lost!' sighed Gran. 'I've been calling him and calling him. I've tapped his dish and rattled his crunchies but he hasn't come in. I think something must have happened to him.'

'Never you mind,' Gran!' said Bone. 'You sit down. I'll make you a pot of tea and then I'll get the gang looking for Percy!'

Before Gran had a chance to say anything, her grandson whizzed past her into the kitchen and put the kettle on.

2

Minutes later, Bone, Omar and Lucy were talking at the end of Woodlands Road.

'I'm going to search the park,' Bone told his friends.

'Check!' said Omar. 'I'll try the back lanes.'

'And I'll look in front gardens,' said Lucy. 'Meet you back here in twenty minutes. Last one back is a soggy chip!'

Bone bombed into the park. He swished past the slide, buzzed round the bushes and flashed through the flower-beds.

'Percy!' he called in his kind-to-cats voice. 'Come on, Percy!' And then, all at once Bone stopped dead on his skates as he noticed that his was not the only voice calling.

A whitehaired man in a brown coat was shouting, 'Tiddles! Where are you?'

A lady with silk violets in her hat was peering under a bush and saying, 'Puss? Here, Puss!'

In fact, the park was packed! Reverend Tricker, the local vicar, was looking for Louise, his pet Siamese. Mrs Beacher, the piano teacher, had lost Lillian, her Abyssinian and P.C. Bloggs had lost Trog, the police station mog.

'Funny!' thought Bone. 'Fancy all those cats going missing at the same time!'

He zipped and zoomed all round the park. He looked in all the places a cat would go and in all the places it wouldn't. He even asked a kindly lady to look in the ladies' loos – but there was no sign of Percy anywhere.

In fact, there was no sign of any cat anywhere.

'Funny!' Bone thought again.

Exactly twenty minutes after they had left Woodlands Road, Bone, Omar and Lucy met there again. They all rushed so fast that they arrived in the same place at the same time, collided with a FOOMF! and landed in a heap the shape of an octopus shaking tentacles with itself.

Omar got up first. He dusted himself down and said, 'I couldn't find Percy anywhere. Funny thing, I met Mrs Ling, Mr Thring and Miss King and they've lost *their* cats too!'

Lucy stood up next. She fiddled with the comb in her hair and said, 'I didn't find Percy either. But strange to say, I met Mr Grey, Mr Faye and Mrs Day and they'd lost *their* cats!'

Just at that moment Bert Mellor, the newspaper seller, started bawling at the far end of the street.

'Read all about it! Local cats disappear! Owners anxious! Police are puzzled!'

Bone, Omar and Lucy looked at each other and frowned.

'Funny!' they all said together.

'Something's going on!' whispered Bone, with a far-off look in his eyes.

'Something peculiar!' murmured Omar, with a further-off look in his eyes.

'Something weird!' said Lucy. Her eyes couldn't be seen because her comb dropped out and her hair fell over her face.

'Search the streets!' cried Bone.

They did. The gang went zinging off all over town. They went down the High Street and up the back streets. They viewed the avenues, peeped in the public swimming baths and glanced in the graveyard. They searched around the cinema, combed the cafes and checked out the stuff the chef had chucked out in the dustbin of the posh restaurant in Southey Street.

They couldn't find a cat anywhere – not so much as a whisker or a paw print.

'I'll tell you something,' said Bone. 'This isn't funny any more – this is a mystery!'

3

Bone and the gang rolled home thoughtfully and, for them, slowly. The mystery of the missing cats was like an itch in a place they couldn't reach to scratch. They were thinking so hard that they didn't pay any attention to where they were going and almost collided with someone. Bone swerved, bumped into Omar who tripped over Lucy and KERLONK! – the three of them ended up on the pavement.

'You stupid young fools!' snarled a voice. 'What do you think you're doing?'

Bone, Omar and Lucy looked up and saw Professor Silas Fletch (the miserable wretch!). Professor Fletch was lean and mean-looking. He was almost bald, but tried to cover it up with the few bits of hair he had left. His head looked like a boiled egg with strands of grey wool stuck on it. His eyes were the colour of frozen dishwater and the frames of his spectacles were made of cold steel. His skin looked as white as aspirin.

'S-sorry!' apologised Bone.

Professor Fletch stared so hard at Bone, Omar and Lucy that his eyes went wrinkly and crinkly at the edges.

'I know you children!' he hissed in a voice that was drier than an old spider's web. 'I've seen you fizzing and whizzing around on your skates! I should like to do some tests on you ...'

'GULP!' went the gang.

'I'd like to put you into one of my famous scientific machines,' went on the Professor, 'where you'd be teased and squeezed, brushed and crushed, starved, carved, tethered and feathered until I'd found just what it is that makes you all so fast and so thin ...' The Professor smiled. It was like a white worm writhing under his nose. 'Then I'd bottle it, sell it as slimming medicine and make bags and bags of lovely, lovely money!'

'R-really?' stammered Bone.

The gang didn't like Professor Fletch, he gave Bone the creeps, Omar the collywobbles and Lucy the heebie-jeebies. Talking to him was as much fun as drinking a glass of frogspawn.

'Well, we must be going!' said Bone.

'We'll be late for tea!' said Omar.

'Let's get out of here!' urged Lucy.

They scrambled to their feet, feeling Professor Fletch's

eyes on them all the time. It gave them the same uncomfortable feeling as a snowball down the back of the neck.

The Professor turned and got into his car. Bone, Omar and Lucy hadn't noticed his car before, but they noticed it now. They couldn't help noticing it.

'It's crazy!' said Bone.

'It's cracked!' said Omar.

'It's well-whacky!' said Lucy.

The car was long and thin and covered with white, silky fur. At the back was a tall, thick aerial that looked like a bushy tail. At the front, the headlamps were blue. The engine started up and made a purring noise. As the car drove away, Bone read its numberplate out loud: 'CATS OOO.'

'Funny!' said Omar and Lucy.

And then they all saw something that made cold feelings run down their spines faster than a small child going downstairs on Christmas morning. Their eyes went like railway tunnels and their mouths opened wide enough to fit in a bunch of bananas sideways.

The boot of Professor Fletch's mad motor car wasn't closed properly. From the open gap in the boot twirled out two tails – one ginger, one black with a white tip.

There was no doubt about it – they were cats' tails.

4

'Whoo!' exclaimed Bone.

'Phew!' snorted Omar.

'It can't be true!' said Lucy. 'Professor Silas Fletch is a world-famous scientist! He can't be behind the cat mystery!'

'He lives in that big mansion on the hill outside town!'

said Omar. 'What would he want with a load of cats?'

Bone scratched his head and frowned suspiciously. 'I wouldn't put anything past the Professor. He's lean and mean and his voice would make a polar bear shiver!'

'But he's famous!' said Lucy. 'Who would believe us if we told them he was pinching people's cats?'

'No one!' grunted Omar.

'This,' said Bone, 'is definitely a job for the Woodlands Road Skate Gang. I say we should go home, have our tea and meet up later. We're going to go to the Professor's mansion and take a look for ourselves!'

'Yeah!' agreed Omar and Lucy.

When he got home, Bone was so excited that he could hardly eat. He went up to his bedroom to wait, but he wasn't good at waiting. When he tried to read, his eyes kept slipping off the page. Every time he looked at his alarm clock, its green numbers seemed to be flashing slower. At last came the sound Bone had been waiting for – the music of the big film starting on TV. Bone knew his mum and dad were dead keen on the film and would hardly notice anything for hours.

Bone slipped out of his bedroom window, glided over the garage roof and climbed down onto the garden path. Then he was off at top speed. He threw some gravel up at Omar's bedroom window, raced down to throw gravel at Lucy's bedroom window and was back in time to see Omar's head appearing.

'I'll be quick, with you in a tick!' Omar whispered.

Bone skated to Lucy's house. She waved at him.

'Just hang on! I won't be long!' she said.

In less than a minute, the gang was off. They went the shadowy way, down dark lanes and up unlit paths. When they heard grown-ups nearby, they ducked into doorways. Being spotted by grown-ups might lead to a lot of awkward questions.

The moon was up by the time they reached Professor Fletch's mansion. The moonlight was bright enough to read the notice on the wrought-iron gates:

**MANSION MISERABLE
TRESPASSERS WILL BE SMEARED**

'Ooh!' gurgled Omar. 'I don't like the look of this! Creepy! Are you sure this is a good idea, Bone?'

'Crumbs!' cooed Lucy. 'Maybe we should go home and tell our parents about it after all!'

'They'd think we were making it up!' said Bone.

'And how are we going to get in, anyway?' asked Lucy, gazing at the high wall around the grounds.

'You and Omar will have to climb over the wall,' Bone replied. 'I'm going to slip in through a gap in the gate to make sure it's all clear. Meet you in there!'

And so saying, Bone slipped between two railings in the gates. It was scary in the grounds of Mansion Miserable. A pale gravel path led up to a mansion that looked as welcoming as a pit of pythons. Bone moved forwards. His right skate scrunched on the gravel.

All at once there was a whining and a whirring and something came streaking out of the darkness with blazing red eyes and snapping jaws, heading straight for Bone!

5

Bone was sure he was about to be attacked by a savage guard-dog – and it was a funny-looking creature. Its body was metal, it had wheels instead of legs and its eyes were screens with red letters flashing, BARK! BARK!'

Bone froze and the guard-dog stood still. Now that it

was closer, Bone could tell that it was one of Professor Fletch's machines.

'BARK! BARK!' flashed the eyes.

'Er, good boy!' said Bone. 'Good dog!'

'BARK?' flashed the eyes.

'Good dog!' said Bone. 'You hungry, boy?'

'FOOD!' went the eyes. The dog came really close. It had a stubby metal tail which it wagged, making a clacking sound.

'GOOD BOY FOOD!' flashed the red letters.

Bone emptied his pockets. He had a piece of string, an old bus ticket and a few brass screws. When the dog saw the screws, its eyes glowed really bright.

'GOOD BOY FOOD!'

Bone threw the screws onto the ground and the dog started chewing them as though they were toffees.

Omar's special signal-whistle sounded through the dark and Bone followed it. He found Omar and Lucy hidden behind some bushes.

'What's that?' asked Omar, staring at the guard dog.

'Don't worry!' said Bone. 'If we meet any more, give them some metal to chomp on!'

'Which way now?' demanded Lucy.

Bone pointed to some lights shining in the downstairs windows of Mansion Miserable. 'That way!' he said.

Before long, the gang was lurking in the shrubbery, peering in through a window. They saw a long dining hall that was absolutely packed with cats. They covered the floor, the dining table and all the chairs. Some were perched on the suits of armour ranged around the walls and one was dangling from a crystal chandelier.

'There's Percy, my gran's cat!' exclaimed Bone.

'I can see Mrs Banks' Manx cat Max!' shouted Lucy.

'Look!' gaped Omar. 'Isn't that Mrs Curzon's Persian, Astaire, on that chair over there?'

'Professor Fletch must have every single cat in town!' puzzled Bone. 'But why?'

'Perhaps I can explain!' a voice rang out.

The gang turned to see the creepy white figure of Professor Fletch. Before they could dash away, he pressed a button on a remote control unit in his hand. A trapdoor hidden in the earth opened beneath Bone and his pals and they found themselves hurtling down a slippery metal chute.

6

They tumbled into a brightly lit cellar that contained an awesome machine that gleamed. It had dials and wheels, lights and pipes, cogs and knobs and levers. On top of the machine was a large metal funnel, at the bottom two flaps opened out onto two conveyor belts. The machine beeped and meeped and bubbled like a hungry stomach waiting to be fed.

'What style!' gasped Omar.

'What a pile!' boggled Lucy.

'It's totally wild!' squeaked Bone. 'What is it?'

Professor Fletch stepped out from behind the machine. He was wearing his widest, most cheerful smile. It made him look as friendly as a roll of barbed wire.

'This is Kitnap One!' he announced. 'Of all the famous scientific machines I've ever made, this is the best!'

'What does it do?' asked Bone.

'Simple!' replied Professor Fletch. 'I pour cats into the machine at the top and then they come out of the two flaps at the bottom … as fur coats and sausages. With the money I get from selling them, I'm going to build bigger and better machines all over the place. This is just the start of my great kitnapping project! Before long, I'll be the richest man in the world!'

'We must stop him!' shouted Lucy.

'But how?' exclaimed Omar.

'This is a job for the Galloping Giddies!' yelled Bone. Omar and Lucy breathed in sharply. The Galloping Giddies was the most amazing, most difficult and most spectacular feat of rollerskating in the world. It had to be done so quickly that only Bone could do it.

He started slowly, skating around the Professor and his machine in a big circle. Bone skated backwards at times, so that he never turned his back on the scientific fiend.

'Stop this nonsense at once, boy!' snapped Professor Fletch. 'You're my prisoner and there's no escape!'

Bone was going faster now, round and round and round. He went so fast that Professor Fletch began to feel quite dizzy watching him.

'Be still, boy!' he barked.

But Bone kept on going faster. His skates hummed like a top, so loudly that it drowned out the sound of the machine. Bone was going so fast that there seemed to be fifty of him in a big circle going round and round and …

'Oh dear!' croaked Professor Fletch. 'I think I'm going to –'

He fell back in a faint, banged his head on the side of Kitnap One and knocked himself out. The evil professor fell to the floor like a bin-bag filled with blancmange – KER-SPLAM!

It took Bone a minute or two to slow down from the Galloping Giddies. By the time he stopped rolling, the rollers on his skates were worn to a whisper.

'Well done!' shouted Omar and Lucy.

'It was nothing!' Bone panted modestly. 'Just let me get my breath back and I'll nip into town to fetch P.C. Bloggs before Professor Fletch wakes up.'

Omar stepped up and slapped Bone on the back.

'You were crucially wick-ed!' he said.

'I think you were really brave!' Lucy declared. 'If it hadn't been for you, there might have been a cat disaster in this town.'

'Not a cat disaster,' said Bone, 'more like a kit-astrophe!'

dolphin story collections

chosen by **wendy cooling**

1 top secret

stories to keep you guessing by rachel anderson,
andrew matthews, jean richardson, leon rosselson,
hazel townson and jean ure

2 on the run

stories of growing up by melvin burgess, josephine
feeney, alan gibbons, kate petty, chris powling and
sue vyner

3 aliens to earth

stories of strange visitors by eric brown, douglas hill,
helen johnson, hazel townson and sue welford

4 go for goal

soccer stories by alan brown, alan durant, alan
gibbons, michael hardcastle and alan macdonald

5 wild and free

animal stories by rachel anderson, geoffrey malone,
elizabeth pewsey, diana pullein-thompson,
mary rayner and gordon snell

6 weird and wonderful

stories of the unexpected by richard brassey, john gatehouse, adèle geras, alison leonard, helen mccann and hazel townson

7 timewatch

stories of past and future by stephen bowkett, paul bright, alan macdonald, jean richardson, francesca simon and valerie thame

8 stars in your eyes

stories of hopes and dreams by karen hayes, geraldine kaye, jill parkin, jean richardson and jean ure

9 spine chillers

ghost stories by angela bull, marjorie darke, mal lewis jones, roger stevens, hazel townson and john west

10 bad dreams

horror stories by angela bull, john gatehouse, ann halam, colin pearce, jean richardson and sebastian vince